WWF

Wild Friends
Tiger Tricks

By Linda Chapman and Michelle Misra

Illustrated by Rob McPhillips

RED FOX

WWF WILD FRIENDS: TIGER TRICKS

A RED FOX BOOK 978 1 849 41697 9

First Published in Great Britain by Red Fox,
an imprint of Random House Children's Publishers UK
A Random House Group Company

This edition published 2012

1 3 5 7 9 10 8 6 4 2

Copyright © Random House Children's Publishers UK, 2012
Interior Illustrations © Rob McPhillips, 2012

Random House Children's Publishers UK uses the WWF marks under license from
WWF-World Wide Fund for Nature. WWF is not the manufacturer of this product.

WWF-UK is a charity reg'd in England and Wales (no. 1081247) and in Scotland
(no. SC039593) and relies on support from its members and the public. This product is
produced under licence from WWF-UK (World Wide Fund for Nature) Trading Limited,
Godalming, Surrey, GU7 1XR. Thank you for your help.

The Random House Group Limited supports the Forest Stewardship Council (FSC®), the
leading international forest certification organization. Our books carrying the FSC label
are printed on FSC®-certified paper. FSC is the only forest certification scheme endorsed
by the leading environmental organizations, including Greenpeace. Our paper
procurement policy can be found at www.randomhouse.co.uk/environment.

MIX
Paper from
responsible sources
FSC® C016897
www.fsc.org

Set in Bembo MT
Red Fox Books are published by Random House Children's Publishers UK,
61–63 Uxbridge Road, London W5 5SA

www.**randomhousechildrens**.co.uk
www.**randomhouse**.co.uk

Addresses for companies within The Random House Group Limited
can be found at: www.randomhouse.co.uk/offices.htm

THE RANDOM HOUSE GROUP Limited Reg. No. 954009

A CIP catalogue record for this book is available from the British Library.

Printed and bound by CPI Group (UK) Ltd, Croydon, CR0 4YY

"*Maaarooo!*" The strange muffled sound came again, and a shape moved under the tarpaulin.

Emily's heart skipped a beat. There was an animal trapped under there! It must be a cat! She headed towards the sound, picking her way past the sacks and boxes, her feet sticking in the mud.

Reaching the tarpaulin, she took hold of the edge, heaved it up – and gasped. A tiger cub was staring straight at her!

www.randomhousechildrens.co.uk
wwf.org.uk

Meet all of Emily's
WILD FRIENDS

**Turn to page 75 for lots
of information on WWF,
plus some cool activities!**

Stripes

The ginger kitten peeped out from behind
the sofa. His green eyes were enormous in
his little face. "Here, Stripes." Emily knelt on
the carpet and approached her best friend
Molly's new pet. "Come on, don't be silly.
Come out." She edged closer but Stripes just
backed further behind the sofa.

Molly shot a worried look at Emily.
"How are we going to get him out? Maybe
I should go and find some food?"

"You don't need food," said Emily. "If
you want to get a kitten out from a hiding
place you just need to give him something

to chase." She looked round and saw an old fluffy pink fairy wand that belonged to Molly's little sister. "Watch this." Picking it up, she moved the fluffy star along the carpet near the sofa.

Stripes peered out. Seeing the moving toy, his whole body stiffened and he lowered himself down so his tummy was almost touching the floor. Emily waggled it invitingly.

Stripes couldn't resist. Springing out, he started to chase the wand from side to side. "See!" Emily grinned at Molly. She rolled the kitten onto his back. He waved his paws

in the air, scrabbling with his little sharp
claws, and then jumped to his feet. "Here,
you try!"

Molly took the wand and moved it
around. Stripes chased it wildly, pouncing
and jumping. Molly giggled. "Why does he
like it so much?"

"All kittens love chasing things. It's their
way of practising their hunting skills for
when they're older," Emily explained. "Big
cats in the wild do it too."

"You know so much about animals,"
Molly said admiringly.

Emily smiled. She loved animals and was

always reading about them. It helped that
her parents knew loads about them too.
They worked for an organization called
WWF that helped protect endangered
animals. Emily's mum was a photographer
and her dad helped to organize different
WWF projects and wrote articles about
them.

"Are you going away again this summer
holiday?" Molly asked.

"Nope," Emily replied. "Mum's going to
India tomorrow to take some photos in a
reserve there, but as it shouldn't take long,
Dad and I are staying behind."

"Cool, that means you can come round
and play with Stripes lots," said Molly
happily.

Emily grinned. She liked that idea!

"Well," Emily's dad, Mike Oliver,
announced as they set off from Molly's

house in the car a little while later. "I've just had some very exciting news. I've been asked to go to Borneo to write about an orang-utan reservation. I've got to fly out in a few days' time."

Emily stared at him. "Orang-utans! I'd love to see orang-utans in the wild!"

"I'm afraid you're not going to be able to come with me, love," Mr Oliver said, shaking his head. "The region I'll be staying in is quite unsettled, but" – his eyes twinkled – "how does a week in a tiger reserve in India sound instead?"

Emily stared at him. "You mean I get to go with Mum to India?"

Her dad nodded.

"Oh wow!" Emily gasped. *Tigers! She might actually see tigers in the wild!* "I'll have to phone Molly and tell her as soon as I get home!"

"And you'll need to pack," her dad said. "This time tomorrow you'll be at the airport, about to get on a plane!"

Emily was too excited to get to sleep that night. She'd put all the things she would need for her trip in her battered suitcase and it was now beside her bedroom door. As she lay in bed she listened to the familiar trundling sound of her chinchilla's exercise wheel. Cherry lived in an enormous cage in the corner of Emily's room.

Emily got up. It still wasn't properly dark outside and there was enough light for her to see. She undid the cage door. Cherry jumped out of her wheel, scampered up the branch that took up a big part of her cage and jumped out into Emily's outstretched hands, climbing up her arm to perch on her favourite spot – on top of Emily's head!

Emily stroked the chinchilla's soft grey fur. "I'm going away again tomorrow, Cherry," she said. The only bad thing about travelling all the time was having to leave Cherry behind, but her next-door neighbour was always happy to look after her.

Emily carried Cherry over to an enormous map of the world that she had stuck on one wall. Emily had pinned up a photo of an animal on every place she had ever visited. Most of them were in Europe, but on the right-hand-side of the map was a picture of a baby panda cub she'd met in China earlier that year.

"That's where I'm going tomorrow, Cherry." Emily pointed out India. Her heart quickened. "Imagine if I get to meet a tiger!"

The chinchilla squeaked.

Emily smiled. "All right, I can imagine you wouldn't like to meet a tiger!" She pictured a tiger in her mind, prowling around the forests of India. It would be amazing if she could see one in the wild!

Emily stifled a yawn and carefully encouraged Cherry to climb back into her hands. "OK, you can go and play some more," Emily said. "I really should try and get some sleep. It's going to be a long day of travelling tomorrow."

She put Cherry back in her cage. As she snuggled under the duvet she heard the exercise wheel starting up again. Emily shut her eyes and thought about tigers . . .

Lost in happy thoughts, she fell asleep.

Two Travellers

The heat was the first thing that Emily
noticed when she and her mum stepped
out of the plane in Delhi. It was only mid-
morning but the air was so hot it seemed
to hit her like a wall. When they'd left
England it had been a July evening, chilly,
getting dark. Now sunshine blazed down
from the cloudless sky, lighting up the
tarmac and walls of the big international
airport.

The arrivals hall was packed with people
hurrying to and fro, wheeling trolleys,
holding up cardboard notices, greeting

people and shouting. Once they were
outside and in a taxi, Emily found that the
streets were even busier. Every road was
clogged with cars hooting horns, buses
belching out smoke, motorcycles weaving
through the traffic and rickshaw drivers
pedalling along.

There was so much to see – ladies in
brightly coloured saris, men cycling along
with huge bundles of fruit on their bikes,

beggars stopping people and asking for money, and the smells were so different too. It didn't just feel like a different country from England, it felt like a different world!

Emily and her mum were staying in a hotel that night. As they unpacked their things, Mrs Oliver explained the plan for the next day.

"We'll have to be up early to get a train to Jaipur, which is about four hours away. A lady called Anjali, who works for WWF, is going to meet us at the station and drive us on to the village where she lives. It's just outside the tiger reserve. We'll be staying there with her."

"What's the reserve like?" Emily asked curiously.

"Well, it's made up of a central core area and a buffer zone," her mum said. "The core area is strictly controlled so that it's a safe, quiet place for the tigers to live, and the surrounding buffer zone is thick forest. Tourists are allowed to go through the core area on safaris, but *only* if they stay on certain tracks. No one is allowed to hunt in the core area, or even gather firewood or graze animals there. Then there are the local villages outside this area."

"How many tigers are there in the reserve?" Emily asked.

"About fifty cubs and adults. A few years ago poachers killed quite a lot of them, but since then the protection has increased and the numbers are creeping back up."

Emily shuddered at the thought of the poachers.

"The reserve is well protected," Mrs Oliver went on, "but if tigers stray outside the reserve, the poachers try and trap them with snares."

"But aren't there barriers to stop the tigers getting out?" Emily said in surprise.

"No, there aren't any physical barriers around the reserve." Her mum smiled. "Besides, tigers tend to go where they want. Most of the time they stay in the reserve but sometimes, unfortunately, they do wander, and then they can end up in danger."

"Oh, I hope that doesn't happen while we're there," said Emily. "Though I'd love to see one," she added longingly. "As long as it's in the reserve, of course!"

"Me too," smiled her mum.

After a breakfast of masala omelette, a flat bread called a roti, and a delicious platter of mangoes, pineapples

and bananas, Emily and her mum got the train out of Delhi. It chugged through the countryside, passing paddy fields, people planting crops and oxen pulling ploughs. On the country roads there were men driving herds of goats, women selling fruit and handicrafts from roadside stalls, and *lots* of bicycles. Emily stared out, entranced. As they travelled, her mum taught her some words in Hindi, one of the languages that was spoken in the area.

The train finally arrived at Jaipur and they met Anjali for the first time. She was wearing loose khaki trousers and a long-sleeved white top and her dark hair was tied back in a ponytail. She was about the same age as Emily's mum.

"It's lovely to meet you," she said to Mrs Oliver and Emily. "I hope you enjoy your stay here. My house in the village is quite simple."

"I'm sure it will be wonderful," said Mrs Oliver. "Thank you for having us as your guests."

Anjali led them through the car park to her jeep, and soon they were on their way again. Emily sat in the back. "How long will it take us to get to the reserve?" she asked.

"A few hours," said Anjali. "Have you

visited a tiger reserve before, Emily?"

"No," replied Emily.

"Well, there are lots of animals there as well as tigers. It's shut to tourists at the moment – it always closes during July and August because it's the monsoon season and all the rain can make it dangerous for driving around, but we'll be able to go in so your mum can take some photographs. I'll drive you to the village first so you can unpack."

"You're so lucky to live next to a tiger reserve," said Emily.

Anjali smiled. "I think so, but some of the villagers wouldn't agree. Tigers may be beautiful, but when they stray too close to the villages, they kill livestock. Some of the villagers also resent the fact that because of the reserve, they are restricted from using the forest the way they have for years. They see the tigers as pests."

It was hard to imagine people not liking tigers, but Emily could just about understand their reasoning. She wouldn't like it if a wild animal went after Cherry as a tasty snack!

"I've worked here with WWF for five years now," Anjali went on. "We're trying to help the local people learn how to make a living without harming the forest so that they don't resent the reserve and the tigers so much. It would be lovely to think that one day the villagers and tigers could live side by side in harmony."

Emily nodded. She knew what Anjali meant. But for now, she just couldn't wait to arrive at the village and go into the reserve. *Oh, I hope I see a tiger today*, she prayed.

A Strange Noise

At long last they reached Anjali's village.
Pinky-red houses were clustered together
near a fast-flowing river. The road was thick
with mud, and Emily noticed that there
were trees blown down across the road and
that some of the houses had holes in their
thatched roofs.

"We had a storm yesterday," Anjali
explained. She drove very slowly through
the village, smiling and waving at people.

Emily gazed out of the window. Chickens
were pecking in makeshift coops, and cows
were tethered on patches of muddy ground.

The women were grouped together –
hanging out washing, sorting grain, making
bread. Even with the storm damage it
looked like a bustling, lively place.

Anjali stopped the jeep beside a house on
wooden stilts right at the edge of the village
near the forest. The house had a ladder
leading up to the entrance platform. "This is
my house. I had it built when I came here,"
she explained.

"It looks really different from the other
houses," Emily observed.

"Where I come from in Assam, houses

are often built
on stilts," Anjali
explained.
"It stops the
inside being
flooded during
the monsoon
season. I wanted

a house like that here." She turned the
engine off. "Please do come in!"

Emily and her mum carried their bags
up the wooden ladder. Inside, the house was
simple but very pleasant, with low ceilings
and thick walls. There was not much
furniture, but Anjali did have electricity
from a generator, and her own toilet and
bathroom, which she explained was rare in
the village.

Emily went into the room she and her
mum would be sharing and looked out of
the window at the busy village.

Mrs Oliver put her head round the door. "I've just been talking to Anjali about going into the reserve. She says that the roads into the core area are not very safe because of all the rain yesterday. I really do want to go and have a scout round and work out the best place to take photographs, but I think it might be best if you didn't come this time."

"Oh," Emily said in disappointment. She really wanted to go into the forest and look for tigers too.

Mrs Oliver read Emily's thoughts and smiled. "You'll be able to come with me soon. I'm sure we'll see some tigers at some point this week. Don't worry."

Emily sighed, but she knew her mum had work to do. "All right," she said. "I'll be fine here. I can read and do some drawing."

Her mum kissed her. "Thank you for

understanding, sweetheart. Now, come and
have something to eat. Anjali's putting out
lunch and it looks delicious!"

After a lunch of spicy lentil dhal, naan
bread and some fluffy rice washed down
with fresh watermelon juice, Mrs Oliver and
Anjali drove away into the reserve. Emily
waved them off and then went back inside,
but it was too hot in the house and in the
end she took her book outside and sat on
the platform. She gazed around at the
bustling village, the heat making her clothes
stick to her body.
She found her page
in the book she
was reading and
swatted away
a fly that was
buzzing around
her head. As she

did so, she heard a faint throaty mewing sound. What was that? Was it a cat? She looked around but there were no cats in sight.

The sound came again, but this time it went on for longer and had more of a high-pitched wail at the end: "*Maaaroo!*"

Emily cocked her head on one side, listening hard. She peered over the edge of the platform and heard it again. It seemed to be coming from *underneath* the house!

Curiously, Emily went down the steps and looked under the platform. It was dark. She could just see a few sacks and boxes stored on pallets of wood, and an old tarpaulin near the centre that looked like it had been thrown there after the storm.

"*Maaarooo!*" The strange muffled sound came again, and a shape moved under the tarpaulin.

Emily's heart skipped a beat. There was

an animal trapped under there! It must be a cat! She headed towards the sound, picking her way past the sacks and boxes, her feet sticking in the mud.

Reaching the tarpaulin, she took hold of the edge, heaved it up – and gasped. A tiger cub was staring straight at her!

A New Friend

The tiger cub's orange fur was ruffled, her round ears pricked. She had green eyes, enormous round paws and dark chocolate-brown stripes.

"Oh," Emily breathed. The cub stared at her curiously and then put her head on one side and made a huffing noise.

Emily blinked. Was it a warning? But the little tiger seemed friendly.

The cub made the huffing noise again and then looked at Emily expectantly, as if waiting for her to do something.

It must be a greeting, Emily realized. She

knew different animals made different
sounds when they were trying to be
friendly. Crouching down, she copied the
noise. The cub immediately bounded over.
She was about the size of a large cat. Emily
touched her fluffy face and the cub pushed
against her fingers. *I'm stroking a real live
tiger!* Emily realized in amazement.

Suddenly a thought struck her. If the cub
was here, where was the mother?

Emily swung round, half expecting to
see a furious tigress outside the house. She
felt a rush of relief when she saw there was
nothing there.

"Where's your
mum gone?" she
whispered to
the cub. It didn't
make sense.
The cub was so
young that her

mother wouldn't just leave her. Then Emily
remembered the storm. Perhaps the cub had
lost her mother and taken shelter under the
house, getting trapped by the tarpaulin?

"*Mowww!*" the cub said hopefully.

Emily hesitated. The cub sounded hungry.
What should she do? Maybe she should tell
someone in the village? But Anjali had said
that lots of the villagers didn't like tigers.
What if she chose the wrong person? Emily
couldn't bear the thought of anything bad
happening to the little cub.

The tiger miaowed again.

Emily made a decision. She'd keep the
cub until Mum and Anjali came home. She
picked her up. The cub was
heavy in her arms – a
soft warm weight. She
cuddled into Emily's
chest and licked Emily's
cheek with her rough

pink tongue. Emily giggled and carried
her carefully out from under the house and
up the ladder, setting the cub down on the
floor as she shut the door behind her. Seeing
a tassel on the rug, the
little tiger swiped at it
with her paw and batted it
to and fro. Emily grinned.
She was just like Molly's
kitten, Stripes, only
bigger! Oh, if
only her friend
could see her now!

I'd better think of a name for her, thought
Emily. She ran through some names in
her head. Ginger, Marmalade, Tigger . . .
none of them seemed right. The baby tiger
needed an Indian name. Suddenly Emily
remembered one of the Hindi words her
mum had taught her earlier: *Baalika*. It
meant little girl.

She tried it out. "Baalika!"

The cub looked round. Emily smiled. "Now let's get you some milk."

She went to the small fridge in the kitchen at the far side of the room and poured some milk into a bowl.

"There we are," she said. Baalika came trotting over. She looked at the milk and then up at Emily.

Emily realized that Baalika was so little she would still be suckling from her mother and wouldn't be used to feeding or drinking from a bowl. She thought for a moment and then, kneeling down, she put her fingers in the milk and held them up to the cub. Baalika licked hungrily. Emily giggled at the tickling feeling. She lowered

her hand into the milk again. Baalika
continued to lick from Emily's fingers until
finally she gave a deep rumbling purr.
Emily sat back on her heels and Baalika
climbed onto her knee. Emily wrapped
her arms round the tiger cub's warm
body. The cub snuffled at her neck, her
whiskers tickling Emily's skin, and then
gave a contented yawn.
Shutting her eyes,
Baalika fell asleep
in Emily's arms.

Emily hardly
dared move. She
sat as still as she
could on the wooden
floor, unable to believe she was actually
holding a sleeping tiger cub! She gently
stroked Baalika's stripy orange fur, moving
her finger over the cub's fluffy round ears,
making them twitch. Then she traced the

enormous paws with their sheathed claws.
Baalika purred in her sleep and rolled over
on Emily's knee till she was lying on her
back, exposing her creamy tummy. Emily
stroked her fluffy fur. It was hard to imagine
that in a couple of years' time the cub
would be a majestic tigress stalking through
the jungle.

Thinking about that made Emily wonder
again about Baalika's mother. If Baalika
had wandered off, why hadn't her mother
come to find her?

A horrible thought hit Emily. What if she
had been caught by poachers near to the
village? Or hurt in some other way?

Emily hugged Baalika tight. "I'll try and
help you find your mum," she promised the
sleeping baby. "I'll do everything I can."

After a little while, Baalika woke up.
Jumping off Emily's knee, she started to trot

around the living room. Emily stretched her
stiff limbs and stood up too. Baalika sniffed
around in all the corners before coming
back, giving Emily a look as if to say,
"*I want to play!*"

Emily fetched her drawing pad from her
suitcase and scrumpled up a piece of paper.
She rolled it across the floor. The playful cub

leaped over and scrabbled at the paper with
her claws, then chased after it and pounced
again. She was completely adorable!

For the rest of the afternoon, Emily
played with Baalika. It was so much fun
she lost track of time and started with

surprise when she heard the sound of the
jeep drawing up outside the house. Emily
leaped to her feet and opened the door as
her mum and Anjali were getting out of the

car. Emily started to
scramble down the
steps. "Mum! Guess
what's—" She broke
off as she noticed
Anjali talking on
her mobile phone.
She looked angry
as she spoke. Mum
was listening to the
conversation, her face serious.

Emily jumped off the ladder. What was
going on? "Mum?" she asked curiously.

"Just a minute, love," Mrs Oliver said
quickly as Anjali ended the call and turned
to them both.

"They're sending someone straight

away," Anjali said, concern in her voice.

Mrs Oliver's green eyes flashed. "These poachers have to be stopped!"

"What's happened?" Emily asked.

Her mum sighed, running a hand through her hair. "Sorry, Em. Anjali and I were on our way back through the forest and we found a tiger trap near the village. It looks like poachers are at work in this area again."

Emily felt sick. Baalika's mother! What if she had been caught in it!

Mrs Oliver saw her face. "It's OK. The trap was empty. It doesn't look as though they've caught anything yet. Anjali has alerted the wardens on the reserve now and—"

"Mum!" Emily burst out. "I've got something to tell you!"

"What?"

Emily swallowed. What was her mum going to say? "Maybe I should show you instead. Come with me. Quickly!"

She ran ahead of them up the ladder. Her mum and Anjali exchanged curious looks and followed her. Emily stopped in the open doorway. "Baalika!"

"What are we looking at?" her mum said, peering over her shoulder.

Emily's heart flipped. The room was completely empty. The little cub had gone!

Escape!

"Emily?" Mrs Oliver said, in confusion. "What are we looking at?"

"The tiger cub!" Emily said wildly. "She's gone!"

"Tiger cub!" Mrs Oliver and Anjali echoed.

Emily quickly told them everything that had happened.

"How big was she?" Mrs Oliver asked.

Emily showed with her hands.

"She's probably about six weeks old then," Anjali said, looking anxious. "I don't know why the tigress isn't around, but it doesn't look good. No tigress would just wander off and leave her young baby."

"The question is, where is the cub now?" said Mum.

"If she's running loose in the village, we've got to find her!" Anjali replied urgently.

"*Aiiiiiieeeeeee!*" There was a high-pitched scream from outside.

Emily, her mum and Anjali exchanged looks. "I don't think that's going to be hard!" said Mrs Oliver.

They ran outside. From the platform they could see an old lady in an orange sari standing with a spilled basket of mangoes beside her. She was pointing at a nearby coop, where the hens were clucking in alarm. Emily gasped. Baalika was on the far side of the hen coop, outside the wire, her stripy body crouched low to the ground.

The lady grabbed a mango and threw it at the cub. Baalika jumped back in surprise.

The mango split as it hit the ground. Ears pricking curiously, Baalika sniffed at it.

The old lady unleashed a torrent of high-pitched words and threw another mango. Baalika gambolled away, straight between the legs of a nearby ox that was tethered to a tree. The surprised animal gave a startled moo and shied away. Baalika put her ears back and charged on.

Other people had heard the shouting and ran over. Baalika knocked over a basket of bread and then ran straight in front of a man on a bike, causing him to swerve and almost drive into a sagging washing line.

"Oh my goodness!" gasped Anjali. "We'd better do something! She's causing chaos!"

They raced down the ladder. A group of boys started chasing after the cub. Baalika darted from side to side, her ears back in panic, as people jumped at her and tried to catch her.

"Stop it!" cried Emily. She ran after the cub as fast as she could, the breath ragged in her throat, her heart pounding.
Poor Baalika!

Baalika scrambled up a tree, her claws digging into the bark. She stopped on the first thick bough and looked down, her eyes wide and fearful.

People clustered around the tree, every voice raised. Emily reached them. "Please!" she said desperately, pushing her way through. "Let me get her! She knows me."

Anjali and Mrs Oliver were close behind Emily. Anjali started speaking in Hindi and gradually people listened and stepped back. They all looked at Emily.

"Do you think she will come down for you?" Mrs Oliver asked Emily.

She nodded. "It might help if I have some milk though."

Anjali spoke to a lady next to her. The lady hurried into a house and came back with some milk in a bowl.

"*Shukriya*," said Emily, remembering another word her mum had taught her. It meant "thank you". She took the milk and then looked at the cub. She was very conscious of everyone watching her.

"Are you sure you want to try and get her down?" Anjali said softly. "We can phone the tiger reserve. They'll send someone here."

"No, I'll try," said Emily. "She knows me." She hated seeing Baalika looking so scared. "Baalika," she said softly. "Baalika, it's OK."

The cub didn't move. Emily remembered the noise the cub had made when they'd first met and how she'd echoed it. Maybe it would work again? Gently, she huffed out her breath between her lips. The cub's ears pricked. Emily did it again.

Baalika lifted her head and made the sound back.

"Come on, Baalika," Emily whispered. She put her hand in the milk and held it up. The cub's nose twitched. She edged back towards the trunk a little way and then hesitated.

Emily put the milk on the ground and crouched beside it. She put her hand in the milk. Turning round on the branch, Baalika half slithered, half climbed back down the trunk, jumping to the ground and bounding over to Emily. Emily stroked her soft fur as the little

tiger took the milk from her fingers. Once
Baalika had had enough, Emily picked
her up. She reached up and licked Emily's
cheek.

"That was incredible!" Anjali exclaimed.

"Well done, darling," Mrs Oliver said
proudly.

"Let's get this baby back inside," said
Anjali. "Then I'll phone the tiger reserve."

Once back inside the house, Emily
cuddled Baalika while Anjali went into
the bedroom to make the phone call. Mrs

Oliver watched
as Emily and
the little cub
gazed happily
at one another,
Emily softly
stroking
Baalika's
stripy fur.

A few minutes later, Anjali emerged from the bedroom. "They said we should take her to their centre in the reserve. They've had no reports of a tigress having been killed or injured though."

"What . . . what will happen to Baalika if we can't find her mum?" Emily asked. "Will they be able to release her when she's older?"

"I'm afraid not, love." Mrs Oliver looked sadly at the playful cub. "If she's hand-reared she'll become too tame to be released. She'll have to live out her life in a zoo."

"No!" Emily stared at her mum in dismay. She knew zoos usually looked after animals really well, but Baalika had been born in the wild and she should be able to stay here, in her native India, roaming free.

"Let's not worry about that now," her mum said, squeezing her arm. "Let's just get

Baalika to where she can be looked after properly."

"And who knows what's happened," Anjali put in. "Her mother could just be injured or ill in the forest. If she can be found, there's still a chance things could work out OK, Emily."

Emily nodded. Anjali was right. She wasn't going to give up hope just yet. Burying her face in Baalika's fur, she hugged her tight.

The Tiger Reserve

"It won't take long to get there," Anjali said as they drove into the forest. Emily was holding Baalika on her knee. The tiger cub looked around curiously, letting out faint mews of surprise as the open-topped jeep bumped along the uneven surface.

Emily murmured to her soothingly and stroked her.

On either side of the muddy track, tall, slim trees reached up into the sky. The rays of late afternoon sunlight slanted through the trunks, dappling the ground and lighting up the puddles. Everywhere

looked lush and green. Birds called
from the trees and bright
dragonflies darted about
like glittering flying jewels.
"Look – over there!" cried
Mrs Oliver. "A
langur monkey!"
Emily saw a large
monkey with a black
face surrounded by a
white ruff fishing inside
a massive termite
mound at the side of the
track. A troop of smaller black and white
monkeys came racing through the trees
from the right, shrieking loudly. The langur
monkey left the termite mound and swung
after them through the branches.

"There's so much to see!" said Emily in
amazement.

"The forest is an incredible place," agreed

Anjali, stopping the jeep as an animal lumbered out of the trees on the right-hand side. It had a cow-like body with a  small, deer-like head, a dark grey-blue hide and short, upright horns. It stopped in the middle of the road. "Come on, nilgai, out of the way," Anjali said as she waited for it to cross. But the nilgai just stared into the trees, its large ears twitching. Baalika started to struggle in Emily's arms. Opening her mouth, she made a strange yowling noise.

"I don't think she likes the nilgai!" Emily said.

"We'll be past it in a moment," said Anjali. As she spoke, the nilgai lumbered back the way it had come.

Anjali drove on. After a few moments, Baalika relaxed and lay quietly on Emily's lap again. Emily kissed her fluffy head. "Not long now," she promised.

After another ten minutes, Anjali stopped at a green barrier. She entered a code into the small keypad on the side of the gate, and the barrier rose.

"This is the core area of the reserve," Mrs Oliver explained to Emily. "The tiger centre is not too far away."

They soon reached several low white concrete buildings in a sunny clearing.

As they parked, a tall blond man and a woman with short dark hair came out to meet them. Both of them were dressed in loose khaki shorts and T-shirts, and the man was wearing a hat like a cowboy's.

"Emily, this is Tom and Deepa," Mrs Oliver said, jumping out. "They both work here monitoring the tigers for WWF. Deepa's a vet and Tom's a zoologist who studies the tigers."

"Hi," said Emily, over the top of Baalika's head as she got out of the jeep with her arms full of tiger cub.

Tom smiled at her. "So you're our tiger rescuer!"

"What a beautiful cub," said Deepa, coming over. "Hey, baby." She held out her hand but Baalika drew back suspiciously.

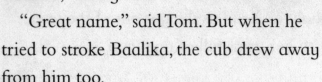

"She's called Baalika," Emily said.

"Great name," said Tom. But when he tried to stroke Baalika, the cub drew away from him too.

"Let's take her to the tiger house," Deepa said. "It's where we deal with any sick animals and orphaned cubs."

"We don't know that Baalika's an orphan yet," said Emily. "Her mum might be alive."

The adults exchanged looks. "It's possible

of course," Tom agreed. "But so far none of
the rangers have reported any injured or
dead tigresses in the reserve, and a tigress
would have to be seriously injured or killed
to lose track of her cub."

"And a cub wouldn't usually lose its
mother," put in Deepa. "Even if cubs get
lost, they're good at finding their way
back to Mum."

"Also, we found that trap near the
village," Mrs Oliver pointed out, looking
worried.

Tom nodded. "I sent a ranger to
dismantle it but there may be other traps."

Emily hugged Baalika
hard. She couldn't bear
to think about her
mother having been
caught by poachers.

"Come on," Deepa
said gently. "The best

thing we can do right now is check Baalika over and make sure she's healthy."

While Tom and Anjali went into the office block to find out if there was any further news from the rangers, Mrs Oliver and Emily went into the tiger house with Deepa. It had a big cage in one corner and an operating table in the middle of the room.

"This is where we examine any injured animals who are sick enough to need

treatment," explained Deepa. "We tend to use this cage inside for any orphaned cubs – there's a big outdoors enclosure a little way from the centre where we can keep adult tigers while they recover from operations. We try to make sure they stay as wild as possible and don't get too used to humans. Now, why don't you put Baalika on the table?"

Emily tried to put the cub down but she ran backwards to avoid Deepa. In the end Emily had to hold her still; only then would she accept Deepa looking her over.

"She's obviously really bonded with you," said Deepa, checking Baalika's eyes and ears. "It's a good sign that she is still suspicious of other humans though. If we're lucky enough to find her mother, then they'll need to return to the wild. If Baalika's too tame, that won't be possible." She took the cub's temperature. "Well, she appears to be in good health," she said as she finished the examination. "Now, why don't you help me settle her into the cage?"

Emily glanced over at the cage. It looked large and empty. She held Baalika a bit tighter. "I wish she could come back with us," she said to her mum.

Mrs Oliver sighed. "I'd love to take her back too, Em, but Deepa's right. Until we know for sure that Baalika is going to have to be hand-reared, we need her to stay as wild as possible. We really can't teach her that humans are all friends and it's OK to come into human houses in case her mother is found. Imagine if she tried that when she's fully grown!"

Emily nodded. Her mum was right. What she wanted more than anything was for

Baalika's mum to be found and the tigress and cub to get back to their home in the wild.

She took Baalika into the cage. It was large enough for a human to stand up in. While the cub padded around, Deepa fetched a large piece of white fluffy Vetbed and bowls of water and milk. Baalika climbed onto Emily's knee and Emily stroked her. Baalika's eyelids drooped and a deep rumbling purr shook her whole body. Emily smiled and kept stroking until the

cub's eyes shut completely
and she fell asleep.
Hearing a faint
clicking noise, Emily
looked up to see her
mum taking photos.
She carefully put Baalika
down on the bed and left the cage. She
stood beside her mum and they both gazed
at the sleeping cub. Baalika looked so
vulnerable, stretched out all on her own.
It seemed so wrong to see her in a cage,
locked up, not roaming free.

Emily felt a lump in her throat. Maybe
that would be Baalika's life from now
on . . . She reached for her mum's hand. "I
want her to be a wild tiger," she said quietly.

Her mum squeezed her fingers. "I know,
love," she said softly. "Me too."

In the Forest

Emily lay on her camp bed and listened
to the faint hum of voices as her mum and
Anjali talked. She tossed and turned as the
image of Baalika all alone in the reserve
crept into her mind. *Oh, please, let there be
some good news about Balika's mum in the
morning,* Emily thought desperately.

She finally fell asleep but woke again just
as the sky was getting light and the birds
were starting to sing. Her mum's regular
breathing was coming from the camp bed
next to her. Pulling her knees to her chest,
Emily thought about the cub. If only there

was something she could do to help find
Baalika's mother. She refused to believe the
tigress had been killed by poachers. She
had to be injured somewhere. Somewhere
outside the reserve where the rangers
couldn't find her.

Frustration gnawed at Emily's stomach.
How could they track her down? A thought
suddenly jumped into her head. Deepa had
said that cubs could find their way back to
their mothers. Maybe Baalika could find
her mum!

But how? How could they explain to
Baalika what they wanted her to do? And
the forest was so big, where would they
start? *I suppose we could drive round and every
so often stop and see if Baalika sensed anything,*
Emily thought. *If she sensed her mum nearby,
she'd probably scrabble and cry and—*

Emily suddenly gasped out loud. Of
course! Baalika *had* done that as they had

driven up to the reserve the day before!
When they'd stopped, Baalika had struggled
and behaved really strangely. Maybe it
hadn't been because of the nilgai; maybe it
was because her
mum had been
nearby!

"Mum!" Emily
cried, jumping off
her bed. "Quick!
You've got to
wake up!"

As soon as Emily had explained what she
had figured out, Mrs Oliver woke Anjali,
who rang Tom.

When she had finished speaking to the
zoologist, Anjali started to pull on her own
clothes and told Emily and Mrs Oliver to
do the same. "We're going to meet Tom and
Deepa and a couple of the rangers at the

point where that nilgai changed its mind about crossing the road. I think you might be on to something here, Emily! Tom's bringing Baalika with him so we can see her reaction."

Soon the three of them were dressed and in the jeep. They drove up the same track as the day before. The birds sounded louder than ever in the early morning.

"So this is where Baalika started behaving strangely," said Mrs Oliver as they stopped. "The question is, if her mum is nearby, which direction should we take?"

Emily stared around. There was something at the back of her mind. The nilgai! It had started crossing the road and then stopped and gone back. Maybe it had sensed danger? The monkeys too! They had come racing from that direction, shrieking and chattering. "I bet it's that way," she said, pointing into the trees to the right of the track. She made to get out of the jeep but her mum grabbed her arm.

"No, Em. It's much too dangerous. We must wait for Tom and the others."

Anjali nodded. "Your mum's right."

Emily waited impatiently. At last Tom's jeep bumped into view and stopped beside them. Tom, Deepa and two rangers who were introduced as Ghalib and Lakshan jumped out. They didn't seem to speak much English but smiled and nodded at Emily and her mum.

"Baalika's in a travelling cage in the

jeep," said Deepa. "Come on, Emily. Let's get her out."

Emily ran to the jeep. Baalika was inside, looking very put out, her ears back, but as soon as she saw Emily, she jumped to her feet and made a delighted half yowl, half miaow.

Emily undid the catch and Baalika leaped straight into her arms. Emily hugged her close. The tiger cub licked her neck and huffed. "You've got to help us find your mum," said Emily, carrying her round to the trees on the right. Baalika suddenly stiffened and made a strange uncertain sound. The next

second she was struggling to get out of
Emily's arms.

"It's OK, let her go," Deepa said. "Let's
see where she leads us."

The cub jumped down, shook herself
and trotted off between the tree trunks.

"Come on!" said Tom. They all hurried
after the cub, stepping over fallen branches
and roots and weaving their way through
the trees. Suddenly Baalika started to
speed up, the trot becoming a gallop.

Emily ran after her. Her mouth felt dry.
She was sure Baalika was leading them
to her mum, but what would they find?
Would the tigress even be alive?

They reached a small clearing and all stopped – Baalika too. Emily caught her breath. A tigress was lying on her side. A snare was caught around her right hind leg. The wire had cut deep into her flesh, blood staining her orange fur. All the vegetation around her had been ripped up as if she had been struggling to get free of the trap.

Emily's heart seemed to stop as she looked at the unmoving animal. "Is she . . . ? Is she . . . ?"

"*Mowwwww!*" Baalika mewed loudly.

The tigress weakly raised her head. Emily

felt relief rush through her.
The tigress's amber eyes
alighted on the cub
and her ears pricked,
but then she saw the
humans too. With the
last of her strength, she
drew back her lips to show

her massive teeth and snarled furiously, ears
flattening as she tried to rise. Exhausted, she
flopped back down.

"She's at the end of her strength but I
think we've just made it here in time," said
Deepa quickly. "If I tranquillize her, we can
free her from the snare then get her back
to the centre for treatment." She crouched
down and opened the medical rucksack
she'd been carrying.

Baalika trotted over to her mother and
gave a small questioning mew. The tigress
lifted her head slightly again. Baalika

pawed at her. "*Mowrw?*"

The mother huffed and then gently licked her baby. Baalika nuzzled against her, rubbing the side of her face against her mother's cheek.

"It's going to be all right," Mrs Oliver said in relief.

Tom smiled. "Thanks to you, Emily. Another tiger saved from the poachers."

Emily glanced at her mum and saw pride glowing in her eyes.

"Well done, sweetheart," Mrs Oliver said softly. "The tigers have got a lot to thank you for."

The team swung into action. Once the tigress had been tranquillized, they cut off the snare and took her back to the centre, where Deepa treated her for dehydration, and

cleaned and stitched up the wound. It was
deep but Deepa was confident the tigress was
going to be OK. Afterwards, she was taken to
the outside enclosure a little way away from
the centre to recover. Baalika was put in with
her too. Emily watched as the cub pawed
at her mother, trying to get her to wake up.
When she didn't respond, Baalika simply
cuddled up and fell fast asleep between her
mum's paws. Emily smiled.

By the afternoon, the tigress was already
showing signs of recovery. When Emily went
to check on her with her mum and Deepa,
she found the tigress sitting
up, licking Baalika,
cleaning her ears
and eyes. The cub
squirmed away but
her mother grabbed
her by the scruff of
the neck and pulled

her back. Baalika looked very disgruntled, but finally her mum was finished. She rolled over onto her back and Baalika climbed onto her tummy.

"How long will they have to stay here?" Emily asked Deepa.

"Not too long. I just want to make sure the wound is healing all right and then they can go back into the wild." Deepa smiled. "I'm afraid you'll have to stop handling Baalika now – her mum won't like it, and we need to make sure they both stay as wild as possible."

Emily nodded. Although she had loved cuddling and looking after Baalika, what she wanted most of all was for the cub to be able to roam free.

"You'll have plenty of other things to do to fill your time anyway," said Mrs Oliver, squeezing her shoulder. "You haven't forgotten that I'm supposed to be here working, taking photos of the other tigers in the reserve, have you? Seeing as you seem to be the tiger expert, how do you fancy tracking down some of them with me?"

"Yes please!" Emily said with a grin.

The rest of their week in India flew by. Every day Emily checked on Baalika and her mum. The tigress was making great progress and it was lovely watching her roll round and play with her cub like an oversized cat with a kitten. Emily saw other tigers in the forest with her mum and Tom

too. It was exciting to track them down
and see the other animals that lived in
the reserve – she even saw three elephants
one day!

On their last day, Deepa decided that the
time had come to set Baalika and her mum
free. While Baalika's mother was occupied
with eating, the gate was opened. Everyone
watched from a safe distance away in the
jeep.

At first, neither mother nor cub realized
that the gate was open, but then Baalika
stepped through cautiously and called to
her mother. The tigress was resting, but
hearing Baalika's cry, she got to her feet
and prowled across the enclosure. Stepping

Take a look at some of the pictures that inspired this story

Indian tiger (Panthera tigris tigris) two month old cub. Image No: 112405 © Martin Harvey / WWF-Canon

A two month-old Indian tiger cub.

A fully-grown tiger, drinking from a stream
at Kanha National Park, India.

out through the gate, she looked around.
She was majestic, her powerful muscles
rippling under her striped coat, her amber
eyes glowing, her tail just swishing slightly
at the tip.

Emily held her breath – what was she
going to do? For a moment the tigress
looked over at the jeep, but then she picked
Baalika up by the scruff of the neck and
walked proudly away into the forest.

Mrs Oliver's camera clicked over and over again. "Look at this!" She showed Emily one of the shots she had taken on her camera

screen. "You'll have to have a copy for your bedroom wall."

"It's perfect!" Emily said, wondering what Molly would say when she showed her a photo of a giant-sized Stripes!

The tigress put Baalika down and walked on, blending into the forest shadows. For a moment, the little cub looked back towards the enclosure and Emily, and then with a happy "*mowww!*" she trotted after her mother into the trees.

"Goodbye, Baalika," Emily whispered with a smile. The tigers were finally back where they belonged – happy, wild and free.

**Read on for lots of amazing
tiger facts, fun puzzles
and more about WWF**

Tiger (Panthera tigris) on a tree, India. Image No: 257491 © Vivek R. Sinha / WWF-Canon

Bengal Tiger Fact File

Best feature: Their distinctive orange and black fur. No two tigers have the same pattern on their coats — their fur is as individual as human fingerprints!

Size: A Bengal tiger can measure between two and three metres from head to tail, and weigh up to 300kg.

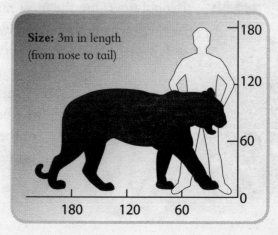

Size: 3m in length (from nose to tail)

Favourite food: Tigers are carnivores and eat other small and medium sized mammals like deer, wild boar and cattle. A single tiger in the wild can eat up to 40kg of meat in a single sitting!

Home: Three-quarters of the world's Bengal tiger population can be found in India, but there are also smaller groups in Bangladesh, Bhutan, Nepal, China and Myanamar. They generally live in the dry and wet deciduous forests of central and south India, the Terai-Duar grassland and the *sal* forests of the Himalayan foothills of India and Nepal.

Current population: Bengal tigers are the most numerous of all the tiger subspecies, but even so, only as few as 1,850 currently survive in the wild. This is a decrease of nearly 95% since the beginning of the twentieth century.

Breeding and family:
On average, female tigers give birth to two or three cubs every two years, or sometimes every three to four. Their pregnancy lasts around three and a half months, and tiger mothers usually give birth to their cubs in a cave or in dense vegetation. Tiger cubs stay with their mother until they are two years old.

Life span:
Unfortunately, about half of all tiger cubs don't survive past their second birthday, but some adult tigers in the wild have been known to reach the age of 26.

Biggest threat:
The Bengal tiger's habitat is being destroyed by the ever-expanding human population, meaning they have less space to hunt and breed. But the biggest threat to Bengal tigers is the illegal practice of poaching tigers for their skins and for use in traditional Asian medicines.

Bonus fact:
Tigers typically travel between 6-12 miles during just one night's hunting!

Quiz Time!

How closely have you been reading this story?
See if you can answer the questions below, or
read the story again to get the answers.

1. What is the name of Molly's kitten?

2. Where do Emily and her mum travel to from Delhi?

3. How many tigers does Mrs Oliver tell Emily there are in the reserve?

4. What colour are Baalika's eyes?

5. What fruit does the lady in the village throw at Baalika?

6. What's the name of the vet who works on the reserve?

1. Stripes; 2. Jaipur; 3. 50; 4. Green; 5. Mango; 6. Deepa

Word Search

Reading across, up, down and diagonally,
see if you can find all the listed words
in the grid below . . .

A	A	C	V	W	F	R	T	G	B	N	M	I
Z	S	E	T	I	G	E	R	E	Y	G	H	N
F	G	G	R	L	A	S	S	L	A	D	E	D
W	A	R	X	D	V	F	E	E	J	K	L	I
E	R	A	V	L	S	T	R	I	P	E	S	A
R	F	S	N	I	S	B	G	L	I	I	H	T
U	G	S	M	F	T	E	B	A	F	N	A	I
I	H	L	R	E	R	H	R	E	G	D	L	G
K	B	A	R	N	O	J	A	N	N	E	U	U
J	V	N	H	A	B	I	T	A	T	G	T	T
H	A	D	Q	M	Y	G	S	G	V	A	A	A
N	E	N	D	A	N	G	E	R	E	D	M	L
M	W	S	A	M	N	L	S	U	X	M	X	B

TIGER   INDIA   HABITAT   WILDLIFE

GRASSLAND   STRIPES   BENGAL   ENDANGERED

Spot the Difference

Can you spot the five differences between these two tiger pictures?

A

B

1. Monkey added on tree root in picture b. 2. Extra pair of legs in picture b. 3. Tail missing from tiger cub; 4. Flower missing from base of tree; 5. Additional dragonfly in picture b.

Word Scramble

The names of these characters
from the book are all jumbled up.
Can you unscramble them?

LAKABAI

☐☐☐☐☐☐☐

JANLIA

☐☐☐☐☐☐

PEEDA

☐☐☐☐☐

YOMLL

☐☐☐☐☐

LI MORREV

☐☐ ☐☐☐☐☐☐

Lost!

Adventurous Baalika has wandered off and can't find her mum! Can you lead her through the maze to find her way back home?

START

FINISH

Fill the Gaps

Can you choose the right words from the list below to complete this paragraph about the threats to tigers?

Asian medicine
poaching
skins
whiskers

The biggest threat to tigers is_____ .
Tiger bones and other body parts are used in traditional _____. Different tiger parts, including claws, teeth and _____ , are believed to give good luck. There is also a demand for tiger _____ for use in clothing, as decoration.

More about WWF

You're probably familiar with WWF's panda logo,
but did you know that WWF . . .

- Is the world's leading conservation organization.

- Was set up in 1961 (when TV was still black and white!).

- Works with lots of different people around the world, including governments, businesses and individuals, to make a difference to the world we live in.

- Is a charity and most of their money comes from members and supporters.

WWF's aim

The planet is our most precious resource and we need to take care of it! WWF want to build a future where people live in harmony with nature.

WWF are working towards this by:

- Protecting the natural world.

- Helping to limit climate change and find ways to help people deal with the impacts of it.

- Helping to change the way we live, so that the world's natural resources (like water and trees) are used more carefully, so they last for future generations.

Three young cubs Sumatra, Indonesia
Image No: 13297 © Alain Compost / WWF-Canon

What do WWF do?

Conservation – Protect rare species of wild animals and plants as well as important ecosystems found in forests, rivers and seas.

Climate change – They don't just tackle the causes of global warming, but also the impacts of climate change on communities and environments.

Sustainability – Help to change the way we all live, particularly in richer developed countries like the UK, including decisions about what we eat, buy and use for fuel.

How can I help WWF?

There are lots of ways you can take action in your own home to help protect our beautiful planet and the people and animals that live on it. Here are a few ideas to get you started ...

Buy sustainable

One of the biggest threats to a lot of wildlife, including the giant panda, is loss of habitat. This is often from people cutting down trees to use in paper or wood products, or to make way for roads, and clearing areas to use for farming.

You can help stop this by only buying products that are sustainably farmed, or wood and paper products from sustainable forests.

So when you're out shopping with your mum or dad, look for:

- **Certified paper and wood products** (look for the FSC logo to tell if something is certified or not)

- **Products made from certified sustainable palm oil** (look for the RSPO logo to be sure that they are certified)

If your local shops don't stock these products – ask them why!

Reduce, reuse, recycle!

Households in the UK send 18 million tonnes of rubbish to landfill yearly. That's more than any other country in Europe!

Top five tips to reduce waste

Why don't you do some of these over a week and see how much less rubbish you throw away than normal?

Take a reuseable bag when you go to the shops, instead of picking up a new one.

Take any clothes, shoes, books or toys you don't want any more to a charity shop.

Clean out old food jars and pots to use for storage.

Get creative with your rubbish and make a kitchen-roll penguin.

Make postcards by cutting old birthday and Christmas cards in half, and give them to your friends.

"Go Wild!"

The way we live can affect people, wildlife and habitats all around the world. Making small but important changes to the way we act really can help to save polar bears in the Arctic or orang-utans in Borneo and Sumatra.

And this is what the Go Wild club is all about. It's your chance to learn more about some of the animals and habitats that we're working to protect. It's also about discovering what you can do in your own home to help look after the natural world.

By joining WWF's Go Wild club at *wwf.org.uk/gowildjoin*, you will recieve a member's pack and magazines that will take you on an incredible journey around the world, meeting some amazing animals and individuals. You'll find out what life's like for them and the threats they face to their environments.

As well as getting lots of Go Wild goodies, being a member means that you help WWF to continue their work. Join today and explore your wild side!

Don't miss Emily's adventure with adorable panda cub Li, in the first Wild Friends story . . .

Read on for a sneak peek!

Exciting News!

Emily rested her pencil on the desk.
The other children at her table were still
copying the map of Great Britain from the
whiteboard at the front of the classroom.
Pushing her dark brown hair behind her
ears, Emily took a piece of scrap paper
and began to draw a panda. She sketched
a round body and head, coloured the little
ears in black and drew dark circles around
the eyes. She then added a stick of bamboo
in the panda's paws. She was concentrating
so hard she jumped when she heard her
teacher's voice behind her.

"Hmm," said Miss Haynes. "Pandas, Emily? I'm not sure *they're* found wild in the British Isles."

Emily blushed guiltily. "Sorry, Miss Haynes. It's just that I'm going to see them with my mum and dad in the summer holidays – in the mountains of China." Excitement bubbled up through her as she thought of what her parents had told her that morning before school.

Everyone on Emily's table looked surprised. The only person who didn't was Molly, Emily's best friend. Emily had told her the news as soon as she had got in.

"Oh wow! You're going to China?" said Anna across the table.

"Cool!" said Ben.

Miss Haynes clapped her hands for silence. "Everyone, take a break from your maps for a moment. This is very exciting news – Emily's going to China in the holidays. So, are your mum and dad going there because of work, Emily?"

Emily nodded. "They work for WWF . . ."

"WWF is an organization that helps endangered animals and protects the natural world," Miss Haynes explained for anyone who didn't know. "Your mother's a wildlife photographer, isn't she?"

"Yes, and Dad writes articles for the annual newsletter and gets involved with setting up projects," Emily finished. "They've been asked to go to China for a week, although I'm not quite sure why."

"What an adventure!" Miss Haynes went to the computer and, with a bit of quick typing and a few clicks of the mouse, she got the WWF website up on the whiteboard and went to the giant panda section. Immediately a picture came up of a panda climbing a tree. He looked so cuddly there

Giant Panda

was a chorus of "ahhs".

"He looks just like a teddy bear!" called Anna.

"Pandas *are* part of the bear family, Anna," said Miss Haynes, clicking on another picture of a panda sitting in the snow eating bamboo. "At one time people thought they were more similar to raccoons because of their black and white colouring but research has shown that they are definitely bears. So, what do you know about pandas, Emily?"

Emily grinned. "Lots!"

Miss Haynes, just like everyone in the class, knew that Emily was completely animal mad. She spent all her time reading animal books and magazines, drawing animals and looking at them on the Internet. "Well, they're very rare," Emily started to explain. "Only between one and two thousand are left in the world. They eat bamboo, but with the bamboo forests being cut down they have less food. And they sometimes get caught in traps that poachers set to catch other animals."

The class grew serious. "That's horrible," said Jack.

"Poachers should be stopped," said one of the other boys angrily.

Emily completely agreed. "WWF are trying to stop them," she explained. "They're creating reserves where the pandas can live. Places where they are safe and there's lots of bamboo – pandas eat for fourteen hours a day!"

"Wish I was a panda!" grinned Jack.

"You'd have to eat bamboo," Molly reminded him.

Jack pulled a face. "Oh yeah."

"That's all very

interesting, Emily," said Miss Haynes. "Now, why don't we have a look at some more pictures?"

A second later, a picture of the most adorable baby panda filled the whiteboard screen.

Everyone squealed.

"Maybe you'll meet a panda cub, Emily," said Molly.

"I'd have to be really lucky for that — pandas don't have cubs very often so they're very rare. Not only that, but pandas are usually quite shy." Emily grinned. "Knowing my luck, I'll probably just see a whole load of panda poo!"

Anna pulled a face. "OK, maybe you're not so lucky to be going after all!"

"Pandas poo a lot," Emily told everyone enthusiastically. "When there are surveys of pandas, the researchers have to pick up the panda
poo and look inside it."

There was a chorus of disgusted exclamations.

"Gross!"

"Ew!"

"OK, Emily. I think that's enough information for now," said Miss Haynes hastily.

Emily sat down happily. She knew one

thing. She didn't care if she had to wade through a *lake* of panda poo if it meant she got to see a real panda in the wild! She just couldn't wait for the summer holidays to start!

For more fun, games
and wild stories, visit
wwf.org.uk

WWF

Indian tiger (Panthera tigris tigris) two month old cub. Image No: 112404 © Martin Harvey / WWF-Canon

A young tiger cub hiding in the grass.

These close-up portraits of tigers give a sense of just how powerful they are.

Look at the size of his paws!

A tiger seeking shade from the fierce India sun.

the amur leopard;

and the Indian elephant

India is home to many wild animals including . . .

the Sambar deer;

the snow leopard;

A picture of a devastating sand storm in Rajasthan, northwest India.